Don't tell lies, Lucy!

A cautionary tale

Phil Roxbee Cox

Illustrated by Jan McCafferty

Edited by Jenny Tyler
Designed by Non Figg

This is Lucy.

Lucy often tells lies.

Once, Lucy tore her T-shirt.

Once, Lucy broke a window.

Once, Lucy made a big 'SPLASH!'

Once, Lucy did some drawing on her bedroom wall.

"It wasn't me," said Lucy.
"A famous artist came to stay."

"Don't tell lies,
Lucy!"
...said her Auntie May.

Lucy's borrowed Paul's bike.

She rides into a tree.

"It wasn't my fault, Paul.
A bandit jumped in front of me!"

Paul runs off angrily to find their family.

"There'll be no more lying, Lucy!

We can't take it anymore!"

"But I'm *not* lying," Lucy lies.
She stomps her foot upon the floor.

She runs from room...

to room...

to room...

slamming every door.

While Lucy's sulking on her bed

and told she must behave...

The others hurry through the door...

...but Lucy's going to stay.

"You are lying, Dad," she shouts.

"I don't believe a word you say!"

Which is how the GREAT BIG WAVE COMES...

...to wash Lucy far away.

"That's the trouble with those who lie," Dad says to Auntie Bea.

"They think the rest of us lie too."

"Anyone for tea?"